Finding Gold in the Golden Years

Finding Gold in the Golden Years

Ruth Reardon

iUniverse, Inc.
Bloomington

Finding Gold in the Golden Years

iUniverse books may be ordered through booksellers or by contacting:

iUniverse
1663 Liberty Drive
Bloomington, IN 47403
www.iuniverse.com
1-800-Authors (1-800-288-4677)

ISBN: 978-1-4620-3597-7 (sc)
ISBN: 978-1-4620-3599-1 (hc)
ISBN: 978-1-4620-3598-4 (ebk)

Printed in the United States of America

iUniverse rev. date: 09/07/2011

Dedicated to my sister, Jean Richmond Bulman, in gratitude for over 80 years as devoted sister and close friend.

She deserves deep respect for the way she has found the gold in the Golden Years, especially given the challenges of Parkinson's disease.

By courage, faith, and love she keeps giving that gold away. Through the years she has enriched many lives, including mine.

FOREWORD

The themes and experiences in this story are realistic and typical of the elderly years.

However it definitely is not a biography or autobiography. All characters and events are purely fictitious. The first person is used only in order that the reader may identify with either sex.

The book is written with touches of allegory and imagination throughout.

An informal colloquial or conversational tone, typical of journal writing, is used.

The gold that is looked for represents what really matters in life. Nuggets shine in struggles, and losses, as well as in hope, fulfillment and enjoyment of life's gifts.

Homespun philosophy and reflections are given by the adult, the five year old great grandson, and many others.

Where Did The Years Go!

I can not believe it!
Bright candles on top of my cake told all.
I was "elderly!" I'm not ready for this!
Going from kindergarten to grade school,
High school, then college, was exciting!
Middle age was not always joyful—but still was o.k.
Never thought that *I'd* be in elderly years!
What are they like? Can't define them alone—
They're part of *all* the years . . . always are with us.
The past asks for continued attention,
Keeps popping up its head.
The future impatiently beckons us on.
The "now" demands priority place!
I'm labeled—there's no turning back.
Where have I been all of these years? Why?
Was pushed ahead by busyness, busyness, busyness.
Many choices were made somehow *for* me—
By events and by life itself.
It was like the proverbial snowball
That grew just by rolling down hill.
Where did the years go?
Went in many directions. Did not just disappear.
They blended into "me," molding, rearranging "me."
They did not "go." They remain within.

Letting Go

What is ahead? For many it's retirement from work.
This does not seem to come suddenly.
It's a process, starting long before it happens.
We talk, talk, talk about it.
We think, think, think about it!
Talking out loud seems to push us on—gently.
We so bravely plan out the date. Postpone it.
Plan another, quite convinced "this is it."
Still find ourselves postponing again.
I myself set and changed dates so many times
My employer threatened to fire me—
To get it all over with once and for all.
Guess we're afraid that losing our work
Means losing . . . ourselves. It does not.
We're not retiring from being the person we are.
Life is not over. We are not over.
It hurts though, really does, knowing another
Will be taking over our place,
A place we had made to fit *us*, no one else.
We feel we're betraying our work,
By handing it over to somebody else—
A *younger* somebody else.
Grieving is a must, and can not be denied.
It's hard to "let go" but at some point we must.
For me that point is right now.
I have given the date. I will keep it.

One More Time

The last day of work was traumatic.
Time went by so slowly. The clock barely moved.
Family called to ask how I was doing.
"O.K" was such a lie.
I removed all the pictures, awards, from the walls.
Boxed my paper weights, calendars, papers.
The room became unfamiliar. My desk not mine.
I could leave at noon, my boss had said,
But being so conscientious—I stayed.
To be alone, I shut the door to my office.
Looked out the window at the hurrying town,
Watched one more time people sitting on benches,
Feeding the pigeons, buying food from the vendors.
I thought back on all my past years . . .
Where did I really succeed in my roles
At work, and at home, in community?
What difference did I make being here?
If time were turned back,
Would I still make the same choices?
This was all too overwhelming for me.
I ate the last piece of candy in my glass candy dish.
Finally opened the door and went out . . .
Came back in for a final goodbye.
I took the stairs, so those people in the elevator
Would not see me like this, so upset.
I'd say my farewells at the soon coming party.

Goodbye

It was celebration and goodbye time.
Walked into the grand hall with the family.
Could hardly believe how nervous I felt.
We were duly impressed with the glass chandeliers,
Elegant white tablecloths, fancy dishes and flowers!
The band announced loudly my presence.
I did not know quite *how* to feel or act.
Happy for freedom? Sad to leave friends?
Decided to handle all feelings "tomorrow."
Everyone came over to greet me—
Told stories they remembered—mostly amusing.
"I'll miss you so much, Jane." I hugged her.
(She made the coffee for us each day—so crucial.)
The meal was just super—must have been costly.
Not in the budget—not my problem though now.
Next came the speeches, all about me.
I was called most predictable, best keeper of rules,
One who never missed work, conscientious, serious.
Sounded like a real boring person.
I did like the award for "most caring."
Back home I looked in the mirror—white hair,
Wrinkles, age spots; yes, I looked elderly.
The party was great—though not perfect.
One co-worker was missing. I said "good" to myself.
I was happy, with my gift, scrapbook, and friends.
I felt very tired. And it wasn't yet ten o'clock.

I Have The Time

I woke up next morning. (Always a *good* thing.)
And here I am, drinking my third cup of coffee,
Wearing jeans, and sneakers and worn red sweater,
Sitting by the long window, at the kitchen table—
The one with the blue checked tablecloth.
It's been there since my beloved one died.
(The cloth has withstood lots of washings.)
I could get another, but this one belongs. It is "ours."
How I love every inch of this home,
Full of rich memories, happy, unhappy . . . all kinds.
It's right on our beautiful Main St.—
A street with Colonial homes and historic buildings—
Some built in the sixteen hundreds.
What stories they could tell!
It's a patriotic town.
For the 4th of July celebration Main St. was painted
With red, white, and blue lines down the middle.
The many lawns and bushes are well manicured.
There are exquisite gardens, and stately trees.
Right now I'm just thinking—eating a donut.
My collie is staring at me. Why am I home?
I tell him that things have changed.
We'll be seeing a lot more of each other now.
I'm retired and in the so called Golden Years.
Guess I'd better find out what they're like.
I have the time, and of course I like gold!

Not "Over The Hill"

The mailman came up to my door.
"Why all these cards?" he asked me.
"Congratulation cards." I answered. "I retired."
"Wish *I* could" was his comment.
One card told me that I was "over the hill."
I laughed. It was funny but not true at all.
Our "hill" really has no top—
Unless we choose to make one.
We don't have to reach some summit,
Then go right back *down* the other side.
The goal is to keep going "up."
Trails are ready, waiting for us.
They'll be new; we'll miss the familiar,
But go on. We have energy. A lot to still give.
Everyone has to be a trail blazer here.
"Broken branches" and "thorny bushes,"
Large "rocks," "cliffs," to deal with. It will be hard.
Most of all though, we must keep looking "up"—
Hold on to brand new hope.
Believe in the future, believe there *is* gold to find.
My dog licked my hand in approval.

Can't Always Play

Today I began my "search," my "journey"
To learn about elderly life.
No need to travel far off.
The gold, if any, should be nearby.
I enjoyed the quiet, waved "hi" to a neighbor.
Passing one house I said to myself,
"This man is very unusual.
He retired; he doesn't seem to miss his job.
He's always playing golf, wearing a "retired" cap.
His buddies' wives complain.
He constantly calls *their* husbands to join him.
When he's not golfing, the couple is dining out.
He's gained 10 pounds. His poor wife—5.
There has to be a change here. Can't *always* play.
Is he in denial? Afraid of doing "nothing?"
It's not the same for all.
Some sail happily on, out to life's seas,
Living as actively as before.
Still others face a more gradual retirement—
Changing parenting, homemaking roles.
They have losses, endings also,
Losses that lead to beginnings, new paths,
Where hopefully gold awaits."

911 For New Retirees?

I saw my cousin Kay at the bank.
One of the banks which serves coffee.
She had recently retired from teaching 1st grade.
Kay looked completely exhausted today!
Her bright auburn hair was pulled back with elastics.
No lipstick, nail polish; she wore wrinkled clothes.
"You look so tired" I said. "*What* are you doing?"
"Not much" she answered, a little sarcastically,
"Just joining two clubs, buying a new computer,
Redecorating my bedroom, taking senior trips."
"Kay, slow down! You have years ahead!
At this rate, maybe you won't, though.
One would think you're taking a college course
In retirement 101—majoring in *activity*."
She smiled faintly. I think she liked my attention.
"You're right" she sighed. "Working *was* easier.
I'll think about it. I really will!"
Retirement left a void. She's filling it to overflowing.
She may soon drown! Is there a 911 for retirees?
We must not jump on merry-go-rounds,
Enjoying the music but going nowhere.
Horses are nailed right down to the floor.
Can't go anywhere but round and round.
We all need time to think, to choose . . .
No merry-go-round horses should control us!
I'll check on Kay. See that she takes my advice.

Fuzz Balls Or Not

There's always a favorite sweater!
We have 10 in our closet
But reach for that one most every day.
Why? Because it's familiar, comfortable.
People compliment the way we look.
The favorite sweater takes on life,
And becomes a faithful friend,
So we keep wearing it, fuzz balls or not.
Until daughters put it in the bin—
The bin for homeless people.
One daughter of a friend did exactly that!
Her dad made her drive him downtown.
He determined to look for it. Rescue it.
His embarrassed daughter had to watch
As he rummaged frantically.
She pretended to not know him when he called
"I found it" and held it close.
He left a new one in its place.
The older one was his friend, you see,
And you don't get rid of older friends.
You never replace them. You can't.
My favorite sweater is the red one.
My loved one had said blue was my color—
Matched my eyes.
No one notices what my eye color is now,
And red seems to make me feel brighter.

Dust First, Then Vacuum

A recent retiree woke up at 6 a.m.
In a panic he jumped out of bed,
Fearing he'd be late for work.
Then it dawned on him that he'd retired.
No one expected him. No job for him to do.
He could choose to sleep all day—
But really he did *not* so choose.
Having responsibility—being needed—was missed.
So was the security of a title and group.
He wished for a reason to set the alarm clock!
Tried to supervise his wife's housework.
That went over great!
Told her it was best to dust first, *then* vacuum.
He was grieving his losses in his own way.
Finally started looking for odd jobs.
His wife helped him search all the want adds—
Continuously, and hopefully. So hopefully!
Part time work at last gave purpose, structure,
A reason to set the alarm clock again.
His wife had a quiet house once more.
She called her friends to tell them
She could meet for lunch . . . *tomorrow*!
She had missed that as much as he had missed work!

Never Grow "Old"

My cousin Kay's birthday party was quite an affair.
I helped light all the candles on the cake.
We've always had a candle for every year—
Not a single one giving the number of years.
We do risk starting a fire!
I overheard Kay say "I *am* getting old—so old."
Talked to her on the way home.
"Please don't think of yourself as "old!" Just "older."
"Old" sounds so opposite to "new,"
Of being worn out, of not much use.
"Older" links together the past and present
With no assumption of having an ending.
Each day we'll just be "older,"
Accepting the fact that the next day
We'll be just a little more "older" still.
What's one more candle on the cake each year!
Among all the others it won't even be noticed,
But it does give a bit more light of life.
That's good. Better than if we started our life
Having a cake with one hundred candles,
And blew just one out each year,
Watching the number grow smaller and smaller.
Much better to add, than to subtract from, our years.
The candles will be blown out. The wishes live on."
Kay thanked me politely.
"I'll surely remember to never grow "old."

Meet In The Middle

I was so very embarrassed at the Coffee Shop!
With a long, long line behind me,
I couldn't find the right change.
The young clerk kept tapping his fingers.
I smiled "I'm finding you a bigger tip."
He sheepishly smiled back at me—an apology.
He'll learn compassion slowly—as all of us did.
Meanwhile, if he can't understand the way I am,
I'll understand the way *he* is . . .
Close the generation gap a bit.
Where spaces remain we can reach out—
Help each other to cross over a little bit,
Or meet in the middle—
Each willing to take a few steps,
Then look, really look at the other,
Listen, just quietly listen, and think.
It's so easy to keep tuning out others,
Listening only to ourselves.
We may be at different places,
Think different thoughts,
See different "colors" in life.
But the cry of our hearts is the same . . .
Longing to be understood and accepted.
That's the real meeting ground.

My Song

I dreamed last night. Heard music and these words:
"I am your song. God's first thought of you.
With my beginning notes I embraced your parts
Being formed in the womb into *you*.
I came forth as a cry at your birth,
Protesting the losses, injustice we sensed were ahead.
I sang in your smile as you reached out,
Helped shape your delightful wriggles
Into laughs and excitement and giggles.
My voice was heard in your very first sounds,
As you tried to understand, and be understood.
Your faltering baby steps followed my rhythm.
I endured separations, rejections, forgiving anyway.
All pauses, silences, skips, and melodies
Made you into who you were designed to be.
I'll stay with you now in your Golden Years,
Tuned to His perfect pitch—
Harmonizing with others' songs.
Your story (what goes into and out of your life)
Will dance to my music.
Like everyone, you have a song. You *are* a song!"
Those words will sing in my heart forever.
It was a dream, yes, but also more, much more.

A Treasure Hunt?

Another big change has come into my life—
Caring for a five year old great grandson.
His parents have to be away—often.
Not ideal, but it's the way it must be for awhile.
I told the child I had retired.
I was in the Golden Years.
I was going on a search to find out
If there really *is* gold in elderly years.
"A treasure hunt?" His brown eyes widened.
"Well, kind of" I answered.
"This gold is the gold of happiness, love, giving—
Things we can't see with our eyes.
Will you come with me?" "All right" he said,
"If I can keep some and Teddy comes too."
He had no clue about what I meant,
But *any* kind of search for gold sounded exciting.
"Where we will go?" That was very important.
"Right around here—home, and town.
We'll listen and watch, talk with other folks.
I'll be thinking and talking a lot, taking notes.
In about 100 years, together we'll write a book,
On what we see, what we find, what we think.
You'll be a big help and good company!"
He ran off to phone his parents.
They would want to know about *this*!

It's *Ours*

Long years ago the old rocking chair—by the fire—
Was a symbol of elderly life.
Things are much different today.
We're active, creative, often still work.
Elder Services give us great opportunities.
Senior Centers keep us busy.
There are exercise classes, seminars, support groups,
Socials, crafts, transportation,
Lunches, health monitoring . . . and on and on . . .
New offerings keep coming each month.
It's a place to go—to just talk. It's *ours*.
We're welcomed, valued, important.
Our special skills help others there.
The Centers link their communities
With the larger ones of towns and neighborhoods.
They have a wealth of information to give us.
Children and teens come often to help—be friends.
A dish of candy on the reception desk
Gives a message all its own.
When I stop by, with the child,
He thinks the message is "fill your pockets."
I'll have to keep my eye on him.
The old rocking chair can wait.
We're so active we'd just tip it over, anyway!

Who Was That?

The child and I went food shopping.
He wore, as always, his bright green sweater.
(When I wear my red one, we look like Christmas.)
In the cookie aisle *someone* came up to us:
"Imagine seeing you!" she exclaimed.
"Imagine seeing you," I answered.
"You're looking wonderful" she said happily.
"So are you." I answered honestly.
"How's the family?" she looked at the child.
"Wonderful." I introduced my great grandchild.
"It's been such a long time!"
I agreed "I know." Wondered *how* long.
"We must all get together." "Yes, soon," I nodded.
"Say hello to everyone" she added
"You too." We said goodbye.
"Who was that?" the child asked.
"I don't have a clue" I confessed.
"Why didn't you ask her!" He raised his eyebrows.
"I didn't want to admit I forgot her name.
I was afraid she'd think less of me."
This is a problem for us elderly.
We pretend, avoid it, or play word charades.
I decided my pretending was over.
I will stop fearing the opinions of others.
We had indeed found gold—right in the cookie aisle.

Cooking With Love

We went to dinner again at my friend's house.
Though elderly, she cooks with love and enjoyment.
Her food feeds hungry souls as well.
Healing is found in the breaking of bread.
Eyes are opened to truth as in years ago.
Her potato pancakes at Hannukah
Are the best in town.
She seizes the moment to teach guests.
Whenever roast lamb is served
She reminds us of the first Passover meal
When bitter herbs were used—and their message.
Tonight, as her famous rolls were passed around,
She told how manna was sent each day
By Jehova Jirah, "our Great Provider."
She related ways in which water was given
To quench all kinds of thirst.
She made water seem like champagne!
We also get doggie bags—with bagels.
No wonder the child comes gladly.
She tells him she *loves* his green sweater.
Says "goodbye" adding "Shalom."
Explains it means peace, blessing, all needs met.
No wonder that I, too, "come gladly!"

Options A Or B?

When something in life disappears
We deal with the loss. That is good,
But often we keep staring at the void.
The hole, will be filled—be sure of that!
Filled with *what* is up to us.
We can't just sit by the edge,
Expecting the winds of life will blow *something* in,
Something we might, or might not, like.
We have two options—A or B.
A—fill the hole with ashes of our despair,
Maybe put up a sign "beware of hazardous waste."
B—fill the hole with acceptance and hope.
Put up a sign reading "please help yourself."
The listening child raised his eyebrows.
(He does that a lot.)
"Then we'd end up with a hole again."
He looked worried. "Oh no" I assured him—
"We'd keep filling the hole with nuggets to share."
"Oh good." He looked relieved.
"That's better than falling down holes."
I'm not sure how much he understood.
I'll explain more later. He's very bright.
I'm so glad he'll be with me so often.
I think he is too. Teddy's not sure . . .
He's afraid of falling down holes.

She Only Smiled

A beautiful, very ill six year old, in a wheelchair,
(Completely dependent—unable to lift her head.)
Was in the hospital lobby with her parents.
She only smiled at me—I felt eternity near.
Had she been so close it was imprinted?
Without a word she gave me her message—
"Love and trust. It is o.k."
Why to me?
Maybe it was easier to "talk" to a stranger
Than to those grieving so deeply.
For one moment time seemed to stop.
Space disappeared
And we held our own communion service
With an unseen Presence.
I saw more deeply than ever that the weakest life
Is a gift to be treasured—as is *all* life.
My child got close and gave her a nugget.
They smiled at each other as only two children can.
She patted his soft green sweater.
I smiled, through my tears.
So did her parents.
So did the doctor and nurse.
That day she became a part of me . . .
Of all I'll ever be,
And all who *my* life shall touch.

Under The Covers

Two nights ago thunder roared. Lightening flashed.
The child jumped into my bed.
Hid under the covers
Holding Teddy and his flashlight too.
Turned the flashlight on—but *under* the covers.
Didn't want to see what might come!
Covered his ears, kept his eyes shut.
When all was quiet, he returned to his bed.
I was wide awake by then,
Thinking of fears of my own.
I, too, hide under "covers,"
Will not deal with, or see certain troubles—
Hear rumbles of guilt, fear, anger, anxiety.
I let light shine into only safe places I control.
And what are the comforting Teddies *I* clutch?
It all started with childhood trauma.
Memories tagged along with the years,
Affected my body, mind, spirit . . . my life!
There are forces out there trying hard
To keep us from becoming
All we were meant to be.
Would I dare turn the light on our fears?
What would we see? What would we do?

No Time To Go It Alone

Another storm last night! The child arrived on cue!
I made a decision, at last, that fear must go.
We lay on *top* of the blankets.
I held the child's hand very tightly.
Teddy's hands were folded in prayer—
We joined him. It was no time to go it alone.
We kept our eyes *open* when lighting flashed,
Kept our ears *open*, calling the thunder names—
Names like "just bowling balls hitting the pins."
I knew we had to find peace *in the midst* of storms,
Or we'd always be waiting for a storm to end,
Before being able to rest.
The shadows were told *we* were in charge.
We changed our troubled thoughts.
This made some new patterns in our brains.
The child dealt with outside terrors.
I confronted ones hidden inside.
It was our beginning stand against fear.
Will take much time, courage and knowledge—
That's all right.
The One who is Love will help cast out fear—
Send Trust to be near when rumbles are heard.

Losses

Another funeral—Another loss!
Another name to cross out of the address book—
I could use liquid white out.
That's drastic. I'll leave her name alone.
I may highlight it. She highlighted my life!
We expect more and more losses like this.
All of us have faced them since birth—
Loss of the womb, bottle, being carried around,
Loss of home, neighborhood, school, and friends,
And of our first goldfish. Won't forget that one.
Another kind of loss happening often
Is the loss of a life-long dream.
Reality tells us it will never be.
"That's sad" the child said as I read this.
"A merry-go-round ride might help you."
We took one.
I pretended my horse flew up to the clouds.
I tried to say goodbye to my friend,
But found she was still part of me.
Said goodbye to my dream.
It was transformed into one I could fulfill
In everyday life—
Simple—different—but still golden.
Happy music of hope lifted us up.
We stayed on to enjoy three more rides.

To Be His Friend

My great grandson and I watched an older man,
Living next door to me, hire teens to shovel snow.
He must have thought of the years long ago
When, eager for cash, he shoveled all day.
It must hurt now to look out the window,
Seeing a job he did better—before arthritis came.
I heard he always gave generous tips to the teens,
Showing he was still quite successful—well to do.
When the teens left he went out to build a snowman
With *his* own great grandchild
Who laughed and hugged tightly to warm him up
In more than just one way.
We watched them go inside—for hot chocolate?
I said to the child beside me, at our window:
"That snowman they made looks lonely—
Let's make another to be his friend!"
So we did. Wrapped plaid scarves on each one.
Gave both bright orange carrot noses.
The child pretended they said "thank you."
He replied "You're so welcome."
We went inside, ate hot soup at the table—
The one with the blue checked tablecloth.
How I wish his other great grandparent
Could share this with us.
Well, maybe . . . who knows.

Don't Lecture—Just Love

My great grandson came with me
To the great grandparents' group meeting.
(No sitter available.) It was a mistake.
He nudged me at advice he thought I needed.
I nudged him back; he let out "ouch!"
Folks shook their heads at my parenting skills!
The leader gave us a list of do's and don'ts:
"Don't volunteer to chaperon 1st graders
Unless the ratio is one to one.
Don't *ever* help at High School dances.
Do help with homework. Give unconditional love.
Don't criticize a low school grade, or hair style.
Do over feed them and have food traditions.
Don't put "extra" creamers in your pockets.
Do order appetizers; leave generous tips.
Do try to understand who they are,
And who they *think* they are.
Maybe they'll try to understand—you!
Don't lecture, just love. Give a vision of truth.
Do listen, listen, listen. But don't over react!
Do send them home with smiles and hugs.
Do let them stay up beyond bed time.
Don't complain about the noise they make.
They'll grow up . . . your house will be quiet—
Too, too quiet.
Enjoy them, and the noise . . . *now*!"

Needed

I had lunch today with long time friends.
We met at a small quaint restaurant
With strawberries all over everything . . .
On the walls, the shelves, windows, dishes . . .
The couple had just resigned as heads of a charity.
I thought this place would cheer them up.
We sat at a table—once a sewing machine!
"There's so little we can do now." one said.
"Just volunteer a few hours each week.
With so much help needed that can't matter!
Why are we still here in this world!"
"All the "littles" are important." I answered,
(Pleased with a chance to advise. They asked!)
"For instance, a comma, as opposed to a period,
Changes the message within.
A pinch of an herb when cooking
Brings out a special flavor.
One cymbal crash livens a symphony.
In a picture one bit of a color highlights the others.
We're each a gift, bringing life to many.
Why are you here? You're needed, that's why.
You're making a difference. That's not "little."
They both felt a little bit better.
We ordered the favorite strawberry shortcake,
And they felt a whole *lot* better.

Never Mind "Why"

"Can we go to the circus?" the child asked me.
Knowing I needed to "lighten up"—I said "sure."
We watched a clown on a tight rope, balancing.
That balance kept him safe.
The clown did not look up, or down,
But moved straight ahead—his eyes on the goal.
Music was leading him on,
Giving the rhythm for the walk.
I told all this to the child, adding
"That's why we need a song."
He frowned at me, declaring
"We also need to chill out—have fun!
Let's buy some cotton candy—never mind why."
The lady next to me clapped at his words!
I ended up buying cotton candy and drinks
For her and her seven kids. Yes, *seven*!
I learned an expensive lesson.
Like the clown I need balance—
Balance between teaching and having fun.
I have to "play" more, loosen up, relax.
I remember the awards at my party!
Awards for being so serious.
I'm trying—but it's hard in elderly years!
Guess it's time for a weekend away—
No reason "why." Just for fun.
I can't believe I'm actually saying this.

How Can You!

"You're selling your house? How can you!"
Grandchildren objected, in shock.
My brother and sister-in-law had a hard time.
"Downsizing" it's called.
Will we? Won't we? Should we? They worried.
Opinions came from everywhere. Little ones cried.
Now it's Senior Housing. Three rooms. Not seven.
Talk about "togetherness." No space between them!
Boxes are still piled up, full of cherished possessions.
Losses like this must be felt and then grieved.
I know. I know. I am repeating.
If not grieved it will be the same
As trying to sing in a major key
While the background music
Plays in a minor one.
"Home is where the heart is."
Their hearts are at the old address.
In time those hearts will be at home
At both the old and new.
Love will make a pathway between the two.
Later, the "new" will be "old" also.
Both will merge as just one whole—
The past and present—yes, the future too!
Elderly life is a series of mergers, of changes.
Losses and gains appear everywhere,
Changing the flow of life, while changing *us*.

It Will Turn Up

My gardener came inside for a cold drink.
(He's elderly, has arthritis, but does a great job.)
Asked "Did I leave my jacket here last week?"
I laughed—"No. Has it disappeared again?"
"It will turn up." He casually shrugged it off.
He doesn't seem worried about forgetting a lot.
Is not upset when he "blanks out"
On names or places or dates.
Focuses instead on remembering
To care, to help, to smile, to give,
And just forget what he cannot remember.
His jacket's always found . . . somewhere.
(Seems it's lost more than worn, though.)
He wiped the sweat from his sun tanned face.
"I do eat a lot of blueberries you know, for memory.
So many that my skin may turn blue!"
He refuses to think of Alzheimer's disease.
Says he's just getting "old"—he means "older."
However, most of us *do* worry about forgetting
And where that forgetting may lead,
So we do puzzles, exercises, learn new things.
Brains *can* keep growing. I.Q.s *can* increase.
(Wonder how high they *can* go?)
We keep picking blueberries. Freeze them for winter.
By spring we don't want to see one more blueberry
On a bush, in a dish, in a jar, or pie!

Foolish For Children

A group of seniors nearby dress up as clowns.
Visit hospitals wards
To be foolish for children.
Found talents they never knew they had.
Were creative. Used former work skills
As a foundation for creative new ventures.
Dignity is forgotten as they make patients laugh.
Wards are brightened as the clowns play tricks,
Sing, tumble, stumble, visit each room,
Giving soft Teddies to hug.
Pain and fear are forgotten for awhile
As children laugh and giggle,
Amazed by the clowns' funny antics.
It's part of their treatment, the best part of all.
Parents who watch their children's joy
Have tears in their eyes as they say "thanks."
Back at home the clowns wash off the make up,
Take their pills, pay their bills, plan for next time.
There's no curtain between us and the sick,
Us and the poor, us and disaster.
We may have retired from occupations,
But never retire from reaching out.
I was pleased when my great grandchild
Emptied his piggy bank
To make a donation for new hospital toys.

Sharing Tears

It seems all right to share happiness, success,
But not to share sadness, struggles.
Jesus set a better example.
He wanted friends near in Gethsemane.
Often it's not tears that we want to hide—
But it's what is *causing* them.
If tears come out, we fear feelings will follow,
And feelings are hard to share!
Tissues can well absorb the tears.
Sharing could absorb the feelings.
Takes courage. Feels risky.
Though others reach out to help,
The door is in our control.
If we'll open it just a crack,
Others will help us open it wider.
Years ago, as a child, I'd tell parents
"I don't want to talk about it"—
I'd go to my room, crawl under a blanket.
Questions just pushed me further away.
Sharing grows even more difficult as we age.
We want to model "maturity," "self control."
Are too "grownup" to "let down."
Maybe childhood is when my rigidity began.
My great grandchild has no problem here.
He lets feelings out—oh yes! Whenever he wants.
Maybe he'll help me.

Free To Choose

One member of our Senior Coffee Club
Came into the restaurant, depressed.
"I'm trying to fix things for my children—
Trying to straighten them out. No use!"
All of us "jumped" on him:
"You're trying to live your life through them.
It's their life—not yours.
You can't control them. Control is subtle,
Often hidden beneath *our* high hopes.
They must be free to choose.
(Decisions made to please *us* are not theirs.)
No life is lived to the fullest
If another's shadow blocks its light.
We have to let them "go." *We* have to "go."
Support them, yes. Run their life, no!
Warn them of danger, "yes," oversee decisions, "no."
Can't keep pain out of their life!
One thing we *can* do is add consistency
To their inconsistent lives."
We congratulated each other for these thoughts.
Ate more donuts. We'll deal with indigestion later.
Will deal with our children's rebukes—later.
They seem to be having trouble—letting *us* go!

Names On The Back

I've already put names on the backs of my "things."
My best dishes, antiques, furniture, pictures.
They are part of the past, must be part of the future.
Remain as part of the ongoing family.
With each new generation they'll mean more
And will keep us connected through centuries.
The love I leave is better than these.
Each share is important—part of the whole—
The whole of *me*. The whole of the family
I pray will remain as one. Will stay together.
Each one needs the others
Whether they know it or not.
The child kept turning things over. Looking.
I caught him erasing some cousins' names.
I showed him the paintings he loved, of the sea
With his name on the backs.
He smiled. Just needed to know.
Replaced the names he had erased.
I'll also leave my song
And my story. Don't say "oh no!"
I'm aware I repeat.
Helps connect the past and present
So I remember where I was,
And how I got here.
Each time I repeat I understand more.
The family may also, and stop saying "oh no!"

Just The Same?

Finally attended a High School reunion!
After all, a friend was coming from *Europe*.
I walked into the fancy hotel. Full of strangers.
Who *are* these people! At least we have name tags.
Try to fit each one into classes, clubs,
But they're strangers now, mature,
Separated by miles and life's events.
All we share is our age, and four years of the past.
Time has changed us, inside and out.
The teens we knew are hidden in the bodies
Of white haired lawyers, teachers, electricians—
And who are *we* this night?
After dinner and speeches by aged class officers,
We look at old slides. Are they really of us?
When we say "you look just the same,"
It's partly true. Memories help fill the gap.
We remember the voice, the laugh, expressions.
They join the young and older together.
The hall rings out with the old school songs,
But is it us, or the teens we were, who sing?
It's good to feel once more that we belong.
I guess we *will* come again. To hear once more:
"You look just the same."
We'll add with no hesitation "well, so do you!"
In the depth of our hearts we'll *believe* it!

We Can Tell

Especially in elderly years we need, yes, *need*
A primary care doctor who, though limited by time,
Pressured by insurance rules,
Will answer questions,
Explain the diagnosis, treatment,
Even when the waiting room is full.
This doctor sits, at least a little while.
Of course some visits will be hurried.
Emergencies don't choose convenient times.
A little compassion makes up for this.
Words can soften apprehension. Words like
"Good to see you." "We'll beat this."
"Must be hard." "I'm sure this will help."
"You'll feel better soon."
Words do help. Even more helpful is the feeling
The doctor really cares; we can tell.
Our feelings are important. If we're stressed in mind
The body will share that stress and get sick.
When compassion and respect are shown
We're grateful!
In this confusing medical world
We need a primary care doctor who's a center point.
Thank you, all of you, who are that kind of doctor.

Dared Look And Listen

This rainy morning I went up to the attic
To sort, preserve, give away possessions.
This helps me to also sort, preserve, give away
My thoughts, and visions and goals.
A "Must" for the elderly.
I climbed the narrow stairs,
Looked around the half cluttered space.
Found a box with all sorts of things
Saved from my childhood home.
There was a tennis ball, marbles and board game.
I smiled, but then sadness came,
With memories of rejection and loss.
Why the ball? I was cut from the team.
The marbles and board game?
Many times no one would play with me.
Rejection made me reject others
Before they could reject me.
That led to separation and loneliness.
Feelings came up and I dared look and listen.
I recognized, forgave those involved, released them.
Replaced dark thoughts with happier ones.
I know I'm not finished—it's a process,
But I'm on my way.
Brought down the ball, marbles and board game,
To give to the children.

Claiming Our Space

Some of us are like revolving statues,
Bolted in place, claiming our space,
Programmed within. Turning, yes, but not touching,
Keeping our distance. Looking with eyes averted.
We're controlled by what's "appropriate"—
What's "politically correct." We fear rejection.
Can't risk the touching lest we chip ourselves,
Mar the painted finish.
Our smiles have boundaries, measured and firm.
Words are chosen carefully
To protect us and keep the "others" out.
We hear only what we wish to hear.
Could we take out our bolts and nuts?
Risk losing some of *our* share
So we can share with others?
Could we choose to be involved?
To sing to another—listen to *their* song?
Really care what *their* story is?
Could we move off separate pedestals,
Take someone's hand and dance together?
Time is going by so fast!
If we're to change ever, we'd best hurry.
The Golden Years took a long time coming—
But they will be gone very quickly!
It's time to look for the gold in others—
Find it and enjoy it, and enjoy *them*.

As Long As There's Life

One volunteer at the Senior Center
Keeps getting new "parts."
Knee replacements, hearing aids, glasses,
Pacemaker, even a transplant!
He's often discouraged; who can blame him . . .
But he still brightens the Center,
Joking about his "reconstruction."
Says he's like the toy Potato Head.
Doctors keep replacing, rearranging parts.
Sometimes we catch him wiping away a tear.
He ought to be told that's o.k.
It's possible to be sad, and yet be courageous.
Though life is hard, he lives his beliefs.
Replaces negative thoughts with positive ones.
Some of his friends don't believe
There's gold in these Golden Years.
Sadly, they expect to just go "down hill."
But a few, not all, watching this man,
Decide to join in the search for gold.
It's not ever too late to choose.
As long as there is life
There's gold that is ours to claim.
Quality time can make up for a lot.
It outweighs quantity time.

Making, Saving, History

It's time to get all my things in order,
Be ready to "downsize" . . . somewhere—
Don't know where—just know the day will come.
I *have* begun looking through papers,
So heirs won't be lost in a paper maze.
Wish there were a GPS for this!
Have many years of medical records, bills, reports,
News clippings, tax forms, report cards.
What to tear up? To save? To give away?
Took courage just to toss out light bills!
Letters from World War I share a box
With letters from World War II.
I've kept war medals, service awards,
Several folded flags and hundreds of V.F.W. pins.
We say "thanks" to those in uniforms now,
And are grateful for sacrifices, through the years.
Besides military albums I have twelve albums more,
Full of old, very old, snapshots of our relatives.
Need to label them. I've forgotten who they are.
I could make some names up—
But won't confuse future genealogists.
Hopefully *they'll* find out!
We're all linked in an ongoing chain,
Making history, saving history . . . our own!

Heart Prints

We're each "one of a kind."
No finger prints are just like ours.
No heart prints, either.
Our very being is unique. So also are our gifts.
We can't measure or weigh or evaluate them.
Finger prints show identity.
Heart prints show the person.
To be seen, finger prints must be on a *thing*.
Heart prints must touch another's *heart*
To leave a mark.
Our personality matches no other's.
Ask any nurse caring for newborns.
Each cry, each look, is different from the rest.
Each of us has his own reason for being.
Has gifts to fulfill it.
Each has his own "self" to love, to accept,
Not trying to be like someone else.
We're part of an interlocking puzzle,
Adding our gifts, embracing those of others.
No one piece has perfect, smooth edges,
But irregular ones, made to fit in a special spot.
No one can take our place in the "whole."
My great grandson—a teen now—liked hearing that.
We've been on our search for over eight years.
I told him he's wonderful—one of a kind.
He agreed.

Does He Remember My Love?

My brother has Alzheimers.
Last week he put toothpaste in the freezer!
(Not funny when it is *your* brother.)
Got dressed for Sunday church
Where he seems to get special peace.
Waited for his ride. It was not Sunday.
He's getting some nursing care. I'm losing him.
Eighty years will disappear—to where?
When he doesn't know who I am
Does he still remember my love?
I keep saying that I love him, though it hurts
When he just repeats the words back to me.
I'll keep reaching out, loving the brother he was,
Loving the brother he now is.
At the deepest core, they are still the same.
I'll share his frustration, understand his anger,
Cherish the moments the "cloud" lifts off,
And I see him "back."
My great grandson visits often, with me.
Just rambles on and on about his teen life.
I almost see amusement in my brother's eyes.
Maybe he's thinking "what *is* this kid all about!"
He touches the teen's green sweater.
Does its softness bring back a memory?
I think I'll buy him one also.
Maybe it will be a "friend" to keep close.

Laughter And Fun

I was sitting again, in the clinic waiting room—
And I really do mean "waiting."
My granddaughter kept me company,
Reading magazines, watching people. All "older."
A woman, obviously hurting, came in.
Asked "Is this where one joins the army?"
There was a twinkling in her eyes.
If she *had* to be there, she was going to enjoy it.
We laughed "yes—an officer will take our names.
Just need the doctor's signature."
She may have lost quite a lot—but not her humor.
The atmosphere brightened; we all talked *together*.
Blood pressure was lowered, just in time.
We laughed on the short walk home,
Thinking of *me* in the army!
I might have marched, but folks would have stared.
We felt good. Cleaned my house. Organized clutter,
Cooked a real feast for supper.
Left the dishes to wash . . . tomorrow.
Watched an old funny movie instead.
Laughter indeed *is* the best medicine.
We need to have fun. Doctors prescribe it.
Boosts our immune system.
Unbending routines prevent creativity.
But fun must be planned, or maybe won't happen.

Giving And Receiving

We walked with a friend who is nearly blind.
Sees the world as though looking through wax paper.
Depends on others' descriptions.
"How can we help?" I asked. He told us:
"Let *me* hold on to you. Guide, don't push.
Help me, but let me share control.
I've lost physical sight. Must keep my inner sight.
Let that guide my choices and guide my life!
Understand my needs, but first, understand . . . me.
I have a vision and a mission—like everyone.
It's to share my love, purpose, wisdom, my self.
All these *do* touch many, travel on and on.
I can excel in this way, you see.
Everyone has some limitations.
Fulfillment in life is living right *in* them,
But also is rising *above* them.
How can you help me? By leading me, as I ask.
Also, by letting *me* lead *you*—in different ways.
We must give . . . and also receive from each other.
Our greatest gift is not what we have
But who we are!"
I was silent for awhile, absorbing his words,
Absorbing the light of his wisdom.
It shined on our path . . . like gold.
Gold that had already been refined!

The Sun Does Not Fail

Though the sun streams right towards our window
It cannot come in if the shade is kept down.
It could, it would, if we pulled the shade up.
The sun does not fail. It's always there, waiting.
Wants to enter. The shade blocks it out.
There are different kinds of shades—
Lack of love for ourselves, and for others,
Rejection and worry, bitterness and fear . . .
The thickest shade of all is unforgiveness,
The greatest room darkening shade.
I am struggling with this one! It's winning!
Still have resentment towards that one co-worker
Who had made my life unpleasant
And once really betrayed me.
I know I am hurting myself . . . and her,
But am not ready to deal with it yet.
It is easier to think about my great grandson.
He is still angry at a coach he once had.
Why? He'll only say that the coach was mean!
Whenever "forgiveness" is mentioned
He tenses up and changes the subject.
Just like me.

Not Weakness But Strength

My eyes needed special treatment.
Didn't want to be a bother to anyone.
Put the eye drops in myself. Wasted a lot.
Drops ran down over my nose, my cheeks.
Pushed some back into my eyes.
I know, I know, it wasn't at all sanitary!
When I called for a refill the nurse asked
"How *could* you have used so much!"
I just let her guess.
Last year I dragged a branch from my yard.
Tripped and sprained my wrist badly.
Six people said "*I* would have removed it."
We learn the hard way we do need help.
Asking, receiving, takes practice.
We hold on to the way we were
Till sure of who we are now,
And believe that "who" *deserves* help.
The elderly use the words "sorry" too much.
Seem to apologize for just *being* here.
We have to see our own value so others will too,
Stop saying "I'm fine, you're fine, we're all fine!"
Most often we're *not* "fine" alone.
Asking for help is not weakness, but strength.
It's also wisdom and common sense.

Further Than The Store

Finally called the Senior Center for transportation.
(See—I admitted I needed that help!)
I took my seat unhappily on the van.
The others looked so elderly, but I fitted in.
I knew I was going further than the store—
Was starting a journey of dependency . . . .
How long? With whom? Where? How?
I'm losing some control in my life.
At least I can always control my own outlook.
As we drove along I watched people
Walking, driving, hurrying,
Going whenever, wherever they wished.
Do they appreciate the privilege?
I looked away, and smiled "hello" to passengers.
They smiled back. They understood,
Knew the route and were willing to show others.
The pain was lessened as I realized
I was taking the higher route of acceptance,
Traveling with friends—rather friends "to be."
Who knows *where* we might go together!
This might be called an "ending."
I'll call it a "beginning."
Beginnings are just turns in new directions,
As we say goodbye, sadly, to old ones.

All At The Same Time

Earlier today we walked in the rain
To the center of town.
We needed a gift for a child's birthday.
With such a large family
We can celebrate "life" very often.
The town has several unusual stores
With unusual gifts, for all ages.
Suddenly we saw everyone stopping,
All looking up to the sky,
Pointing out the gorgeous rainbow.
We watched, with friends and strangers,
The beauty of the rainbow
As it said "goodbye" to the rain,
"Hello" to the sun.
No words were in the sky.
The rainbow itself is always the message.
Calls all of us to look "up," to see hope.
It draws us together to look to a center
All at the same time.
If we really listen we may hear angels clapping . . .
For the incredible display.
If we really look, we'll catch a glimpse, maybe,
Of the pot of gold,
Before going off in our separate paths
As the rainbow fades away.

Like It Or Not

My teen great grandson is having melt downs.
Wants more freedom when he's with me.
That's not as often now, but still frequently.
His parents expect me to give him limits.
I told him "there *are* rights, wrongs, absolutes, sins.
Like it or not, there are consequences in life.
No one can do what they want all the time."
I lectured and did not feel guilty at all.
"Even you?" he asked slightly sarcastically.
"Even me," I replied, ignoring his tone.
"I don't want to stop at red lights,
But I do for safety and to avoid a fine!
We are also given higher laws to obey.
The good thing is there *is* forgiveness
For all who plead guilty, accept redemption.
The fine has already been paid."
No comment from him on this.
Dealing with parents and me was enough.
We went out to a diner.
I laughed. "We're eating *chicken* nuggets
While we're searching for *gold* ones."
"Well *these* are just served by the waiter," he said.
I did not add that the waiter also *served* a bill.
I thought to myself—we *are* finding gold—
Gold hidden beneath hard rocks. Not easy!

Shalom!

One couple moved to an apartment
In a tall Housing Unit for seniors.
Hardly like the houses they'd lived in before!
They open the door—still half way expecting
To step out into a yard . . .
But there's only a long, long corridor
Between two long, long rows of doors.
An elevator takes them "down"
To go outside to lawns and paths not theirs,
To flowers they did not plant—can't pick.
The couple didn't quite know how to relate
To the residents—
As students in a boarding school?
Close neighbors?
As tourists . . . or relatives? They were fearful.
(Notice how fear shows up everywhere?)
All was soon "colored" by acceptance.
They dealt with things as they *were*,
Not as they wished they were, or as they should be.
Both began to greet neighbors with "Shalom."
As they wished this peace to others
More was received for themselves.
It will take time to adjust . . .
These years it seems we're always "adjusting,"
And "adjusting" never gets easy,
Until *we're* "adjusted" ourselves.

Candles Unite

My mother had a great love for candles—
Even made some, and taught me how.
She lit them at each celebration.
But most of the time she had no reason—
Just lit them. Passed her love for them on.
Candles are more than decorations,
Or for emergencies. They are symbolic—
Not switched on and off, but are lit,
Allowed to flicker naturally.
Candles are loved—all over the world.
There's the Menorah, Christening and
Wedding candles, Advent wreaths,
Paschal candles at Mass,
Tiny birthday candles standing for life.
Candles are a central part of vigils.
They unite us when these dark times come,
For we all have similar candles,
Have the same hope and sing the same songs!
In windows they shine for a vision or cause.
I like their sense of mystery, of "more"—
Tonight I lit another one, with pine tree scent.
My great granddaughter watched silently with me.
The light of the candle was reflected in her eyes . . .
I hope also in her heart.

"Get A Tutor"

Book clubs, seminars, learning new skills
Help keep our senior minds alert.
What works even better is time with a teen!
Mine asks questions about everything under the sun.
He also needs help with homework. I'm lost!
I did go to a class for parents of students,
Students about to take upcoming SAT tests.
I could hardly see the writing on the screen,
Hardly hear the presenter.
Hardly understand what it was all about!
One mother advised me "get a tutor for the teen!"
I didn't ask *that* many questions.
The "final straw" came when I caught a glimpse
Of my former co-worker sitting way in the back,
Looking calm and wise, and innocent.
I was out of there. Disappeared quickly!
I decided to leave homework and test preparations
For his parents, who were home more now anyway.
I'll exercise my mind with puzzles and games.
Meanwhile, for my own self esteem,
I put one of my old honor report cards
On the mantle for all to see!
I feel like sending a copy . . . to "that mother."

Five Hundred Thousand Miles

My friend came over for supper.
Had to get out of his house—he was so angry!
He pounded my blue checked tablecloth.
"My family insisted I no longer should drive!
I taught my daughter years ago to drive,
Risked my very life. Is *this* her thanks?"
I tried to calm him down.
We ate supper and a huge bowl of popcorn.
Watched T.V. until he went home.
I hope they let him mourn this loss!
Since sixteen he's gone where and when he wanted,
In full control of a treasured car.
It started when he turned the key,
Followed where he turned the wheel.
Keys symbolized independence. Symbolized *him*!
About five hundred thousand miles came to an end
With "screeching brakes," "deflated tires."
It was hard to say "goodbye" to this final car.
At last he gave it to charity.
Would not forgive the family.
Back seat driving was how he punished them.
When he rode on the bus he sat up front
To supervise the driver.
One resigned last week. Wonder why?
That's all right. He'll break in "a new one!"
With pleasure.

Not Half A Person

When the Mr. and Mrs.
Becomes just Mr. or Mrs.
We're divided—at least here.
One no longer living. The other, alone.
How can one do what two should do?
Or be what two used to be? Commitment is over.
"Till death do us part" and it did.
We tell ourselves and others
That we're *not* half a person,
But just half of the whole made up of two persons—
A great loss, a wide open space.
One identity gone now—"wife" or "husband."
Another identity added—"widow" or "widower."
We have to fill a new role.
Everything gets changed. Names on documents,
Address labels, tax returns, census forms, bills,
And all the little boxes on all the questionnaires.
Relationships with others aren't the same now.
Friends have to relate to one person, not two.
Otherwise we'd feel left out,
Feel neither "here" nor "there."
But we go on, making adjustments over and over.
Never forgetting the Mr. or Mrs. gone on,
Looking forward to the day we'll see each other,
And hopefully know what boxes to check.
And we'll both have stories to tell—oh yes!

God On Trial

We've seen, in our long life, much suffering, loss,
For young and older, rich and poor.
We're quick to put the blame on God.
Ask "how can a loving God allow all this?
Why? Not fair? I can't and won't believe!"
God gets more "credit" for the "bad"
Than "credit" for the "good!"
We don't have perfect knowledge—
Nor see all life's pieces—past, present, future,
Yet God's on trial for our imperfect picture.
We act like self appointed judge and jury,
Give a "guilty" verdict before all evidence is in,
Pronounce the sentence . . . "you're rejected."
Hopefully, in Golden Years, if not before,
We'll grow in understanding. Get to know Him,
Surrendering to Faith, to Trust.
Declare a mistrial—let Him out of jail.
He'll forgive, share our grief for all the "bad,"
Help us see beyond our present view—
See Faith and Trust be vindicated,
And "why's" no longer asked.

Their Best

The Special Olympic events were held nearby.
The teen and I attended
To cheer on a young friend—and an older one.
(The oldest participant, I heard, is 92!)
We were awed by what we saw.
Watched those living with challenges
Proudly competing, encouraging each other,
Achieving awards, respecting each player.
They were applauded by a crowd who believed
In the human spirit's ability
To rise above, live above, overcoming.
Only some "win" gold, but all win the contest,
For they do their very best.
That's true of top athletes around the world.
They too can do only their best.
Watching these Special Olympic stars
I saw very clearly
That one of their gifts is to inspire us all
To do our best in life.
We cheered till we went home . . . very hoarse,
But with high respect and deeper understanding,
Realizing they need our gifts,
And we need theirs.

What About Mercy?

I used to drive our "late" children
Each time they missed the school bus.
Friends said I should make them walk!
What about having *mercy*?
I'm glad I drove them when I could!
None of them were "spoiled."
At least they got to school on time.
They learned responsibility other ways.
Life's good at that. So were we, their parents.
There were expectations to fulfill—
Or else!
Besides, sooner or later, four out of five
Got their act together. Hurried to catch the bus!
Now, years later, they drive *me* everywhere,
Waiting till I'm ready. (I tend to be late.)
I'm the one needing responsibility these days.
For now I'll just plead for mercy.
Was I right or wrong? The jury's still out on this one.
Perspective grows . . . with age.
I only know I'd rather be wrong for driving
Than wrong that I did not.
I still smile each time I see a school bus.
I think my children do too.

What Happened?

When we return to our childhood home
In thought, or even in person,
The memories are the same, but we've changed,
So changed is also the house.
We know we're back home—but it seems different—
Because we *ourselves* are now different.
No home is ever just only a house.
It's colored, designed, redesigned, by life.
We see scenes we remember,
But we're part now of the audience—
Not stars in the play anymore; mixed feelings!
We become like a child again, confused,
Running from room to room, calling
"Where is the fun? The hopes and people?
What happened?"
The answer is that *life* happened—but it's o.k.
Memories remain in the house and us.
When lonely or hurt, we can return to the house,
Kick off our shoes—curl up in a favorite chair.
If we see shadows of regrets,
"Wish I had," "wish I had not,"
We'll let shine the light of forgiveness.
They'll disappear, replaced by gold.
The home will always be there,
Keeping alive our childhood,
Forever part of our Golden Years.

The Good Old Days

When we get together—as a group,
We end up talking of the good old days.
Reminding each other of many "whens."
"When" there was cream on milk bottles.
Wooden boxes filled with ice blocks.
Rumble seats, running boards.
Children standing by the driver.
Only radios; no T.V. to see.
Played records on victrolas, had player pianos.
A.C. was cold running water over our wrists.
We used ink wells for our pens,
"Wooden eggs" to darn socks,
Garter belts to hold up stockings.
We never forget to include the years
When there were black out curtains,
Rationing, War Bonds, care packages,
Working in vital defense jobs,
Fighting in World War II.
Memories are so special—
Because they include people we loved.
We enjoy our "remember when" times,
But we are left a little sad,
Wishing we could go back—
But only for a day.
We need A.C. and TV!

We've Seen Them

In these days of great medical progress
We're driven to find answers to illness.
We marvel when an unseen Power works.
God heals in ways known and unknown,
Through us and without us.
He holds the answer.
In fact indeed *is* the answer.
I was told of a patient whose treatment failed.
Her doctors had given up hope.
Then God acted, without any protocol!
The team could not explain the healing,
Much less the patient who just prayed "thanks."
God is above our small understanding.
We only get glimpses of "why" and "how."
He's already increased our knowledge and skill,
Opening spiritual, physical, doors of healing.
We believe He'll keep opening more.
Meanwhile, there are discoveries, there is hope.
There are miracles.
We've seen them!

Two Teeny Spiders

The woman who lives in the Cape Cod house—
The one with the bright green shutters,
Had the cleanest house on our street.
It was always spotless, ready for company.
She dusted *every* day. Polished her colonial furniture.
Even the windows shined.
Finally, though, she admitted it was too much.
She was slowing down; getting tired.
Besides, a granddaughter had seen two teeny spiders.
That did it! She decided to get some help.
When a cleaning person came, she watched,
Partly with regret. Partly with relief.
Afterward she found her blue glass collection
Still dusty! Cleaned it with great delight.
She was a better housekeeper.
Her self-esteem was saved.
Doing it all by herself . . . was over.
It was all right to feel that loss.
Losses must be grieved and *then* replaced. I repeat!
A friend came over—taught her how to crochet.
Her afghans are beautiful, outstanding.
She gives them to shelters for the homeless.
Talk about nuggets of gold!
Finding two teeny spiders worked for good!

Like A Warm Fleece Blanket

Lost a brother! Suddenly! I'm devastated.
Through all our years we shared everything—
Parents, family, landmarks, holidays,
And most important, "little things"—like secrets.
No more. What good is a secret if it can't be shared!
Friends try to bring sunshine.
It's too bright for tear filled eyes.
Don't tell me of rainbows right now!
I need to just feel the pain of loss—
Not reject or deny it.
My brother may be at peace. I'm not.
My children stayed close.
Didn't know what to do besides share my hurt.
It was enough. Many are not able to do this—
Often because they've not faced their own hurt.
Just the presence of others
Is like a warm fleece blanket
To cover me so I can hide awhile.
Words now are not really "heard."
They will be welcomed—later on.
At this moment let me shed tears.
Then *later* . . . help me wipe them away.

Out Of The Blue

Received a card today—out of the blue.
Couldn't believe the return address!
It was from the co-worker who hurt me so much.
She had heard I was not well.
The verse on the card said "thinking of you."
I bet that she was! No doubt with guilt!
Part of me wanted to toss it—
The whole matter had been bothering me for years—
Like a shadowing weight on my heart.
Part of me knew it was a call to forgive her.
I myself had failed often—been forgiven each time.
Was expected to pass along that forgiveness.
I made a decision—forgave her once and for all.
So I wouldn't "turn back" I called her,
Thanked her for the card.
I admit I felt no great love for her,
But did feel a lot more brighter
And a lot more free, somehow.
We would talk later . . . about the issues.
I'll keep the shade pulled up.
Bitterness went out the open window.
I breathed forgiveness in.
Watched sunbeams dance on crystal glass,
Making rainbows on the wall.

Keep The Shades Up

Next day I told my great grandson the whole story.
He was very surprised to hear it.
I had hidden unforgiveness well—except from *me*!
He looked interested as I talked.
Understood its importance, and my need.
I could tell he was quite impressed.
He's so sensitive and is a deep thinker.
He seemed preoccupied—troubled, all day.
I did not ask why, did not lecture.
I let him do his own deciding.
After all, he *is* growing up! About to start college.
I may never know the details,
But he did drop hints
That he'd made changes and decisions.
Saturday he casually told me
He was going into town to a game—
Coached by the one he'd called "mean" for years.
I was thankful that I had received the card.
Forgiveness had won—double!
"Shades" became a code between us.
Only we two understood the meaning.
When either of us needed reminding
We'd whisper "keep the shades up."

As My Daughter Is Now

I agreed to go to the emergency room—
Not to be admitted! But here I am!
One set of strangers in the emergency room—
Now another set upstairs.
These strangers were examining me.
No good to hide beneath the sheet—
They just pulled it down.
Asked me personal questions.
"You'll get used to it" the family assured me.
I don't *think* so. I'm not staying *that* long!
This doctor looks like he's in High School.
Who's watching *him*?
I would leave but don't know where my clothes are.
They've hooked me up to machines.
I gave orders to my family—never again call 911!
I remembered the way I felt as a child,
So afraid, in a hospital.
The shots and tests hurt badly,
Opened the door to fear, then anger, control.
The college student reminded me now
That we had faced fear many times and won
With the help of Love and Trust.
My daughter sang me a song about that help.
Strange—I remembered my mother singing,
Just as my daughter is now.

"Cheers"—To The Future

In the hospital I felt completely captive
To the illness, the staff, medicine, machines.
We older ones try to find ways, somehow,
To feel a bit in charge. To at least object.
My way? I didn't like the "nutritious" drink given.
"Doctor's orders" they said. Is that right!
I have "orders" of my own! Refused to drink it.
Considered pouring it into plants—to fool everyone.
Why was I making this such a big issue?
Why not just swallow it? Isn't *that* bad!
I think because it was easier to focus objection
On something simple, concrete.
Easier to deal with that—
Rather than the serious illness itself.
The drink was not the problem—
The reason it sat on my tray *was.*
Once I clarified that I felt better, much better.
Decided to surrender and drink!
I raised the glass with a "cheers—to the future,"
Vowing *not* to surrender to illness though.
I had found a nugget of gold in the hospital bed.
My great grandson gave me another—
He had just become engaged!
Last night!

So Much Loss

I was soon sent to a Nursing Home.
I'll only be here a short while,
But some, of course, are in long term care.
There's so much loss for them—
Independence, homes, privacy, ordinary "life."
Must be hard beyond words to be confined,
To follow routines—to be cared for by strangers.
I asked a nurse about their feelings.
"They feel their losses deeply" she said,
"And are afraid of the future.
We do our best to brighten up their life.
Patients at least are sure of receiving care here.
They're not all alone as they might be at home.
(But of course "there's no place like home.")
We offer activities, music, games and social events.
There are Chaplains who give friendship and faith.
Volunteers come to entertain—children also.
Last week someone brought dogs to pet—
Their tricks made many smile.
However, visitors are the most important.
Each brings himself—also the "outside."
He then *leaves* some of himself and the "outside,"
Because the patient keeps going over the talk.
Makes the visit last, long after goodbyes."
The nurse had to go back to her duties,
But added, with a smile, "so *please* visit often!"

When The Angels Come

A patient, Gwen, learned to recognize footsteps
In the hall of the Nursing Home.
Identifies steps of the doctors, nurses, kitchen staff,
Volunteers, and, most important, visitors.
Afternoons, she puts on lipstick,
And wears a special sweater.
Hopes a visitor's footsteps will stop, come in.
Few do. She sighs "tomorrow?" Still hoping.
Some elderly rarely have visits.
Friends and families are gone or moved far away.
I wish more of us could find the time—
(Where does it hide?) to be the footsteps
Which will stop, turn, go in, and visit.
When the angels come for Gwen
I hope they won't fly, but walk,
Stop at her door, go in and chat.
Wait while she puts on her lipstick and sweater.
Maybe then they'll walk back down the hall
So she can wave goodbye to all,
Showing off her visitors,
Asking them to sign the guest book!
For many long years
She's filled the loneliness hole with hope.
Now, that hope is lighting her path
As she learns to keep step with the angels.

I Still Travel

When my eight year old great granddaughter
Visited me at the Nursing Home,
We walked down the hall to see a friend.
He had been there a long, long time—in bed.
The child told him "I'm sorry you're so shut in."
He replied—"of course I'd rather be home,
But decided long ago to *live* wherever I have to *be*.
"Shut in" does not have to mean "shut out."
I still "travel" around, helping people!"
"Like Peter Pan flying out of windows?" she laughed.
He smiled. "I go by way of prayer.
I "visit" people everywhere
By praying for what they need—for God's help.
If prayer is worth anything at all,
It's worth more than we'll ever know.
I'm confined in body—not in mind.
Life's difficult, yes, difficult, but I hope in God.
He's not a visitor. He lives right here.
Get to know Him now, child
So you won't have to get acquainted
When a crisis comes."
The child hugged him.
He thanked her. "Best medicine I've had today!"
My friend was rich in love, in faith.
He gave her a card with a sunrise scene.
It went under her pillow that night.

A Chance To Talk

After "awhile"—seemed a very long "awhile"—
I was allowed to go home, with much care,
And frequent visits to doctors.
One was funny; at least the doctor thought so.
I spoke . . . my son spoke . . . I spoke . . .
We both added to, or disputed, what the other said!
The doctor paid more attention to what my son said
Than to what *I* tried to say.
He meant well. My son meant well.
My son wants to be part of my care.
I need help now on visits. Am grateful.
However, I really do need a chance to talk!
After all, I do pay the bills, and swallow the pills.
I know my body quite well. I should . . .
I've spent many years inside it.
If I can just give my opinion
I'll give the doctor all the credit
For the diagnosis and treatment that we choose.
I won't send a bill for my consultation fee.
Maybe he'll lower *his* bill to me though—
Or send it to my son,
So he'll feel he *does* have a part in all this.
That's the least I can do!

The Hospital's Heart

I'm back in the hospital . . . *again*.
Such a maze of long corridors, arrows and signs,
Flashing red lights, and beep, beep, beeps.
Codes and doctors' names called out.
Rattling of beds pushed up and down halls.
Patients coming, going, the ambulance sirens.
Interrupted sleep, shift changes, pills, pills, pills!
Seems like one big machine running too fast,
Pulling us with it, dispensing tests and therapy,
Following rules, routines. Causing anxiety.
Through it all we find the hospital has a heart.
We hear its healing beat in caring words and touch,
In concern shown on faces, smiles of hope.
Yes, there *is* a heart. This makes us feel better.
At times that heart needs treatment for *itself*.
Not to worry! Recovery is very quick,
For the hospital heart is the heart of the hospital,
So receives top priority care.
I might as well stay awhile.
Last night I felt sorry for myself.
Didn't think the nurse heard,
But found a new box of tissues on my tray,
And a golden nugget.
Have no idea where it came from.
Didn't look for any. Sometimes they just appear.

Who's The President

The newest specialist asked me
"Who's the president?"
I felt like saying "Lincoln"
But didn't dare take chances.
As I left the office I couldn't resist—
Asked how the Quantum Theory
Relates to the science of medicine.
He didn't answer and acted busy indeed.
I don't think he'll ask the president thing again—
(He knows now I'm still quite aware of the world
Despite advanced age.)
But if he should, I'll name the last ten
And who the next should be.
In future years new specialists may ask again—
By then I may very well answer "Lincoln."
And may very well believe it.
When I told the great grandson about this
He started learning lists of our presidents,
Just in case. You never know.
As I told you, he's very bright.
Has mostly *my* family's genes.
At least *he* knows that I know who the president is!

Tears And Laughter

When I came home from the rehab this time,
A walker came with me. I hate it!
Have to maneuver, step with care, depend on it.
My brain goes fast, but not my legs now!
Mind and body used to work together—no more.
Is it the walker's fault or mine?
I'd like to throw the walker out the window,
Fly away, myself!
"Since you want to fly away . . .
You could pretend the walker has wings."
My son tried hard to make me laugh. I didn't.
Told him to go away—leave me alone.
I was exhausted, and angry. He felt sorry, apologized.
We laughed as the dog barked at the walker.
He sure knew trouble when he saw it!
Tears are so close to laughter
That we can quickly change one to the other.
So we might as well laugh.
My great grandson let little ones paint the walker
With very bright rainbow colors!
Now I must buy another for my outside use!
At least I can laugh. I'm not as serious.
My friends at my work years ago should see me now!

Baby Shoes . . . In A Vase?

Yesterday was rough, very rough.
The door to the storage unit was locked
With a numbered key for what *was* my life.
My furniture, except for a few favorites,
Were all piled together—on top of each other.
Chairs I once sat on, lamps that gave light,
Tables where the family ate, talked, played games.
Pictures faced down—showing names of people
Who would someday possess them.
All the unplugged clocks told different times!
How did the baby shoes get inside a vase?
Is this what my life has come to?
They say it will be only for "awhile."
I feel like a part of me
Was also locked in for "awhile"—
To keep my things company? They don't need me.
Who *does*?
I walked away, holding the arm of a son.
Was he leading me, or I leading him?
Which ever—we were very close.
We both had seen not the furniture only,
But also the memories—all "topsy turvy" too.
It left us disoriented and a little "lost."
There must have been some gold hidden there
But neither of us could find it.

So Upside Down

So here I am—starting down a new path.
Really now, how many *can* there be?
It's a path I never considered—not ever!
Living in one of the families' home!
Life had been so exciting through the years.
Retirement, new ventures, challenges, fun—
Then sickness came—completely uninvited.
Brought hospitals, rehabs, nursing homes, losses.
I had seen healings, and years of good health.
Now I'm home—rather, in a child's home.
I miss my own home.
They say this will be just for "awhile."
Have heard *that* one before!
It all seems so upside down.
I'm supposed to care for them, aren't I?
My few belongings, not stored, came too—
Like my rocking chair—and blue checked tablecloth.
They chose this option as best for everyone.
I'm grateful but fear being "a burden."
(Fear always looks for an open door to enter.)
It's *their* home. *Their* life style, *their* routine.
I never signed any contract for this,
Unless I skipped the small print!
Everything's *theirs*. Come to think of it though,
This choice for me was *theirs* too. I felt better.

Pinched Chocolates

The little ones come often to my room,
Thinking I am asleep.
They open my box of chocolates—take two—
Replace the box, giggling softly.
Actually think that they're fooling me!
Don't they realize that I am still smart?
Don't they see that each "stolen" piece
Leaves a tell-tale space?
I could offer them the candy.
It's more fun, though, to play the game.
Only problem is they pinch three or four
Until they find a caramel.
The pinched ones are left for me.
Must be finger prints on them—
These children will never be good at crime!
Often they ask to hear my song.
Are they doing penance for the chocolates?
Later, perhaps, their own songs, at least parts,
Will blend with mine. The choice must be theirs.
Why don't I ask for boxes of all caramels?
Because I've come to like the pinched candy.
Wonder if their parents know? Do they pinch too?
We never completely grow up. Thank goodness.

Signs On The Path

Sometimes we elderly are just worn out.
Everything looks cloudy—or dark,
Despite all our efforts to look "up."
What's the use of walking on—
Can't even find the path for Pete's sake!
Where are we going? Do we want to?
Why not stop, turn around, and forget it!
It's all too painful, too hard!
That's when Another's hand grasps ours.
Leaves in it a golden nugget—wet from tears—
Gold in the shape of a crucifix. Refined by love.
In the dawning light of morning
We see we've been right on the path.
It had led through a lonely garden of grief,
Through thorns, piercing our skin,
Leaving drops of blood.
It led up a hill where we tripped over rugged wood,
Underneath the black sky where a battle was won.
Now the path is in a green meadow,
Beside a pool of still water.
We drink and lie down to rest awhile.
Looking back we see signs on the path
That Someone had walked it before us.
Someone had walked it with us.
Someone will keep walking with us.

Biting Off Heads

I told my daughter I didn't want her cheese soufflé!
It's not one of her better meals,
And she makes it often.
Then I made a bigger mistake—
Suggested she ask her sister how *she* makes it.
This sent her off to a movie—a thriller.
I should have eaten . . . some.
I'm hungry now.
Did she give the soufflé to the grateful dog?
Forgiving is high on her list, however.
She won't let me starve till breakfast.
She'll bring me supper—and maybe cream puffs,
One for me, one for the great granddaughter.
That child got in trouble herself yesterday.
Friends brought gingerbread men for the family.
She ate all the heads right off!
Wonder whose heads they were?
Or did she just like frosting?
Today I feel like biting off heads myself.
Not just for the frosting!
Usually I see *gold dust* on the walkway.
Today it looks like tree pollen,
And I'm allergic to that.
What's this got to do with soufflé? Don't know.
There's a lot I don't know these days.

At Least I *Have* Feet

My daughter washed my feet today.
I, who taught her how to wash her own,
Sat silently, accepting the help.
I always had said, when offers like this came,
"Thanks—but I can do it by myself."
Independence is tied to our self worth.
Losing it is tough. Is ruthless.
I'm challenged, and I do not like it at all!
But what's the alternative?
(And I don't mean dirty feet.)
There's more involved here than what is seen. Hurt.
Maybe gratitude for all I have will deal with that hurt.
At least I have feet and know that I do!
I have someone willing to wash them—
So I'll try to smile and say "thank you."
My daughter will know I mean "thank you."
For . . . everything. Even her cheese soufflé.
Everyone seems to agree it's good, very good
That my feet get washed! We'll leave it there.
My mood brightened up; we all laughed
When the dog tipped over the basin of water.
Covered with soap suds he slid around and around.
I wrapped him in towels and held him close.
We comforted each other.

Back To The Past

The family's talking more about "long ago."
Our minds jump from the present to the past,
Triggered by something happening, or said.
Memories—happy, sad or confused—came up.
I found myself saying "I'm sorry" real often.
They said "It's o.k." many times,
Then we'd let it go.
All sons and daughters told of doing wrong things.
"You never knew" they said, smiling.
(That's what *they* think!) I just said "that's ok."
We forgave ourselves, each other, and God.
I suggested we better ask God to forgive *us*!
There were also some disagreements.
We each saw through our own paradigm.
Also, time, and we, had altered facts, and memory.
"Why's," were a favorite topic,
And God was a favorite target -
Why did sickness and tragedy happen!
A little great granddaughter was listening one day.
That night I heard her pray:
"*I'm* not mad at you, God, like the others."
She wanted no guilt by association. Wise child.
Sometime soon she and I will sit together
And we'll talk . . .
We'll solve all the deep problems. Don't I wish!

Not Childish But Childlike

As I enjoy the children around me I realize
There's a child still within us.
He's been quieted, ignored, denied,
But has always forgiven.
Once in awhile he'll try to reach us,
Play on our heart strings.
At times we've enjoyed him, but then felt foolish.
Dare we face him?
It's time to let him laugh, show us his hurts.
Time to wipe away his tears. Hug him close.
Find again . . . . the child. Let her live. She belongs.
Be proud of her. Tell her she's beautiful. Love her.
Let her dance. She's been waiting on tip toes!
She'll not make us childish, but childlike.
Free her from our mature control.
Receive her gifts she's been waiting to share.
The child wants to come out of the past.
Tells us she's not just a memory.
She was born with a compass and light—
Will help us become more like her,
A child who alone can enter the Kingdom.
One of her missions is to lead us.
One of our missions, especially now
In the Golden Years,
Is to follow.

No "Same Old Days"

A child showed me his new kaleidoscope.
(I had enjoyed many in my own childhood.)
I turned it around and around. Patterns moved.
Colors and shapes of each "sparkle" stayed the same.
However, the pattern changed with the turning,
As each bead moved and touched one another.
Isn't that typical of our lives?
Situations, feelings and groups keep changing.
So therefore do the designs we are in.
No day is ever the same as another.
Our interactions move life itself . . .
Make it flow in many directions.
When there are no people near us,
Our thoughts, attitudes, and memories
Are what can change the pictures.
There doesn't *have* to be any "same old" days!
Moving the kaleidoscope brings change.
Hope and a future lie ahead.
Life moves all the time and so do we.
We find rest in knowing another Hand
Moves the kaleidoscope too.
We make the patterns together,
Always awesome. Always unique.

Left Out

They're all meeting tonight.
Need to talk about plans for me.
I would like to be a fly on the wall!
It will be as it was years ago.
Ron and Debbie will mediate—
Hannah and Calvin will dominate—
Ann won't see any problems to be solved.
Their spouses will be supportive.
Each will see through their own glasses,
"Colored" through the years,
But remaining the same at heart.
They're reacting to losing an independent parent.
Next time I'll ask to have any meeting *here*.
I must keep some control—give it little by little.
It's best given, not taken by necessity.
A little one was angry. He was not invited.
Pizza would be served. His most favorite food.
I told him to look for gold—the good—in it.
He *actually* asked "why don't you!"
I laughed after he left to play.
Was pleased with his free expression,
Pleased with how my sense of humor has increased.
Not pleased *I*, too, was left out tonight.
I may feed the dog the family's prime rib.
Just maybe.

Still The Parent

In this change of family taking care of me
I'll try to be sure no child of mine
Will ever turn into the parent.
Life long relationships can't be erased.
We'll remain the same, though situations change.
There is, of course, the *role* reversal.
If I become more needy
They'll have to act as parent.
It must be *acting* and not *being*.
Even my weakness
Won't take away this basic truth.
If it did, we'd lose *ourselves*.
My daughter sighed at this word "lose."
I assured her we would never "lose" each other.
My children and I are too close for that!
Just then we heard the ring of the ice cream truck.
She ran off to get popsicles, as in years before.
Her sister joined her with four little ones
Who had no money either.
They ran back to me for the money,
As they did when they were young.
Guess things won't change too much now.
I'm still the parent—
At least wherever the ice cream truck stops.

Who's In Charge?

My nephew raised his voice to me! He shouted!
I had walked upstairs, against orders.
People outside could hear him, I'm sure.
So what! He's not perfect, nor am I.
No one has it "all together."
Next time I might shout back. No, I won't.
He was right, frightened I would fall.
Fear and anger get mixed up.
Fear usually starts the problem: anger follows.
Adjusting to any kind of change is hard.
Takes me time and thought and strength.
I guess I was trying to test things out,
See who *was* in charge here—
How dependent I had become—
Where could I just say "no."
I told my nephew I was sorry.
Would obey the doctor's orders.
I must be held to standards I once gave them,
Not allowed to use illness to manipulate.
I asked my nephew if I should miss dessert.
He said "no"—brought me two.
The dog thought one was for him. It wasn't.
The next week my nephew filled the window boxes,
Outside my window, with my favorite plants.
A wonderful surprise.

Caregivers Need Care

"Of course you're going away" I told my daughter.
"One of your brothers or sisters will take over.
The change will do you good."
I added "the change will do *me* good, also."
Didn't mean it. She knows that. But it worked.
That evening she shared her vacation plans.
The support group she and the family attends
Makes it clear that caregivers need care too.
The group means a lot . . . and is helpful.
There's coffee and cake. No one counts calories.
Each understands the rewards and the problems
Caregiving brings. They listen to each other,
Learn it's o.k. to be tired of it all,
To lose patience, sometimes,
To not be a perfect caregiver.
It doesn't mean any less love.
It's safe to let feelings out at the meeting.
Together they can laugh at things
They would not laugh at, alone.
The purpose is support, leaning on each other.
Members go home convinced
If others can do it, then so can they . . .
And they do!

I'll Always Be A Part

Why does everything happen at once?
There's so much going on! But it's wonderful.
I've been feeling a little stronger.
Our young friend came to show us the video
Of his recent Bar Mitzvah; It was impressive!
Another, yes, another, new baby was born.
At the Baby Naming service
I gave her a soft pink Teddy.
In the pocket were eighteen dollars.
I had learned that in Jewish tradition
The number eighteen symbolizes "chai" or "life."
Next, we celebrated my great grandson's graduation.
The party was held right here—what a day!
The gardens were blooming.
The sun shined brightly.
Crepe paper decorated everything—even the dog.
People filled the whole yard. Filled the house too.
Young musicians—with guitars, played and sang.
His parents were *so* very proud.
I met his fiancé—I fell in love with her also!
He posed in cap and gown with everyone, even me.
We two sat inside in front of a window
With the shade pulled way up.
I was thankful to be a part of such *life*,
And knew I will always remain a part.

Always A Mixture

Couldn't dance at my great grandson's wedding,
But I was there!
It was one of the highlights of my entire life.
Then it was *my* birthday . . . again!
The co-worker arrived with a gift.
The dog licked her hand—a very good sign.
My great grandson piled cheese soufflé on her plate.
I, and his wife were watching, so he stopped.
I loved all my gifts, but my favorite
Was one from my children,
A small toy model of a school bus!
Was the party a picture perfect event? Oh no.
A box of chocolates had disappeared.
A littlest one threw up. Was she the culprit?
The doctor called—scheduled additional tests.
My nephew announced he had just lost his job.
There's always a mixture of darkness and light.
To be poetic . . .
The most beautiful pictures of mountain ranges
Show shadows and sun, both at the same time.
The co-worker danced with my great grandson.
He slipped a nugget into my pocket.
I slipped it later into the co-worker's pocket!
Guests left with balloons. Set them free,
Free to dance with the stars up high.

It's Been 100 years!

My great grandson came to visit today, announcing
"You promised me when I was five years old
We'd write a book. It's time. Been 100 years."
I didn't feel that old—I mean "older,"
But was not about to argue the point!
That was that. We began. Read over all my notes.
We smiled, laughed, felt sad—tore up a few pages!
Like a pro he asked "What is our theme?"
Fortunately I had a very concise answer:
"The years themselves were not golden—oh no!
However, there certainly *was* gold *within* them.
To desire that gold, search, find, refine it,
Seems to be the vision, the mission, of these years.
Isn't *that* the theme for our book?"
"It most certainly is. You summed it up well."
We agreed to keep our book simple, conversational.
Basically just use my notes, revised, here and there.
There would be gaps in time.
I was not consistent, but so be it.
The book would be like a journal,
With some allegory, imagination, and inspiration.
The notes tell our story, and those of others,
With home spun philosophy.
My daughter was proud of our progress. So were we!

Where's The Gold?

The next day my great grandson arrived early.
We sorted some more, arranged sequences,
Chose priorities, corrected spelling.
Put the notes in *very* Free Verse form
To make words flow with some rhythm,
A little more like a song.
After working a long time, I was tired. Very tired.
Told my great grandson to go home; come again.
"Just a minute" he objected.
"We collected *lots* of nuggets. Where *are* they?"
He knew the answer.
He was teasing.
"Oh," I replied. "Remember—we gave them away.
The gold is in the giving. You know that."
"But you promised me I could keep some
If I came along." He pretended to pout.
"But you *have*," I laughed. "Look in your heart!
There's a lot of gold in there now,
As there is in mine. We're *very* rich."
He winked.
Went home to his pregnant wife.
Yes . . . isn't it just wonderful?
Some babies are born with a silver spoon.
This baby will come with a gold one.
I've already ordered a tiny green sweater
And a soft, smiling Teddy of course!

What And Where Was The Gold

We continued to write whenever we could.
Felt we needed to sum up
What gold is, and where we found it.
We described the gold . . .
As the becoming all we were meant to be,
As closing gaps between us and others, us and God,
Taking down walls.
(Walls made of gold are still walls, and separate.)
We had learned gold was the healing of fear,
Caring, sharing, love, forgiveness.
It was also knowledge and wisdom.
Knowledge is separate pieces.
Wisdom makes them a picture.
Gold was in children, our song, and hope.
Where did we find this gold on our search?
In everyday life, making the common uncommon.
In rainbows, sunsets, sunrises, mountains and seas.
In illness, in challenges, overcoming.
The gold was right in our thoughts and decisions,
In simplicity of truth. (*We* complicate things!)
We saw it in our dog's devotion.
In a school bus, chocolate, even cheese soufflé!
"And don't forget cotton candy."
He raised his eyebrows, laughing.
"Never." I said, with a sigh and a smile.
I had found lasting gold that day.

Ribbons On Each Child

Life has been quiet—we finished "the book!"
Really! Took a lot of time and hard work.
We copied more notes, revised, added new thoughts
And finally we had "the book."
People seem to like it. *We* do!
My search for gold was re-lived; that brought peace.
My strength may have faded—my faith is strong.
Life is more precious. Hope keeps me singing.
Family and friends seemed to have joined my search.
Everyone sings my song *with* me!
Little ones bring pictures to cheer me up.
The room looks like an art exhibition.
My daughter puts ribbons on each painting,
For all deserve prizes. All are given with love.
She pins ribbons on each child.
They are the real winners.
That tells me my family will keep finding gold,
Long before their own Golden Years.
Often I sit with a child in the large recliner
Where I tell stories with lessons tucked in.
My great grandson sees through it,
Raising his eyebrows and winking.
Truth is gaining a stronghold. They don't know it—
Just the super wise young adult.
I pray the Truth will guide the children
Through all the years ahead.

Forever And Ever

Another great granddaughter started kindergarten.
She spends rainy afternoons "playing" with me.
I asked if she'd like to search for gold
Right here in my room.
She smiled. "I'd like that, if I can bring Teddy
And keep some of the gold." (Shades of yesteryear.)
What a gift to me! Yet another new beginning.
I'll find gold through the eyes of a child again.
There will be nuggets in hugs and coloring books,
Gold in listening to each other and sharing tears.
We will ask for the dress up trunk—and pretend!
I'll sing my song, and she'll learn hers.
What a team we will be—
"Older" adult, little girl, sleepy dog, and a Teddy.
(*Everyone* will be welcomed to visit, join us.)
I'll help her want to "keep the shades up."
She'll help me to just believe . . . like a child.
My search will go on, here, and beyond,
Forever and ever and ever.
The child gave me a hug. Teddy smiled.
The dog wagged his tail in agreement.
We looked out the window at an awesome sunset.
Tomorrow will come . . .
With an awesome *sunrise*.

ACKNOWLEDGEMENTS

I am deeply grateful to all those who participated in various and numerous ways towards the production of this book. Special appreciation goes to my daughter, Beth Vangel, whose extraordinary patience, wisdom and support helped guide this from initial concept through to completion.

Thanks also to Michael Vangel, Deneen Castriano, Frances and Paul O'Brien, Nancy Hansberry, Dr. Martin Iser, Barbara Greenglass, Miriam Patrice McKeon, Virginia VanMeter, Barbara Geary, Jennifer VanMeter, Kathryn Belyea, Ellen Lim, George and Cindy Frode, and Katherine Ells.

The book reflects many gifts of knowledge and wisdom received through the years from countless pastors, teachers, mentors, as well as truly wonderful children, family members, and friends. I sincerely appreciate each and every one.

BIOGRAPHY

Ruth Reardon, mother of four children, nineteen grandchildren, and eight great grandchildren, is the author of three books published by the C.R. Gibson Co.: *Listening To The Littlest; Listen To My Feelings*; and *Listening To A Teenager*. For twenty-five years she served as an Early Intervention Developmental Specialist under the Mass. Departments of Public and Mental Health. She was privileged to learn much from the lives of hundreds of families facing and overcoming special challenges.

Ruth attended Wheaton College, (Mass.) Bridgewater State College and graduated from Gordon College.